The Quarry

The Quarry

Clare Littleford

CRIME EXPRESS

The Quarry
by Clare Littleford

Published by Crime Express in 2008
Crime Express is an imprint of
Five Leaves Publications,
PO Box 8786, Nottingham NG1 9AW
www.fiveleaves.co.uk

ISBN: 978 1 905512 42 3

Crime Express 5

Five Leaves acknowledges financial support
from Arts Council England

Five Leaves is a member of Inpress
(www.inpressbooks.co.uk),
representing independent publishers

Typesetting and design:
Four Sheets Design and Print Ltd
Printed in Great Britain

1.

The last of the day's customers is finishing up his coffee when Jenny Carter's mobile rings.

It's been a long, slow day; one of those days when the clock's second hand seems to falter on its circuit. Jenny is sitting on a stool at the counter, rush-hour traffic reports playing on the radio as she totals the day's takings. Outside, the light is fading fast, washing the colour from the sky.

Coming through from the kitchen, Sue gives an exaggerated sigh and hauls herself onto the other stool. "I'll be glad to get home tonight," she says, and laughs.

Sue's spent the whole day — the whole of the last week, it seems — telling Jenny about her plans for tonight; how she can't wait to scrub the café smells from her hair, the grease from her skin, slip into something glamorous. Jenny can't remember the last time she wore something glamorous herself, or went out on the town, even with Nick; she's surprised to realise that the idea doesn't appeal. The joy of being a mother; she'd only spend the whole evening thinking of home, anyway. She smiles, and opens her mouth to tell Sue to get off, she can lock up alone tonight.

And that's when Jenny's mobile rings. The vibrate rattles against the melomine. She picks it up, puts it to her ear. "Hello?" she says, and a thin, frightened little voice responds:

"Mummy, Mummy, I'm in Quarry Woods."

The blood drains from Jenny's face. She feels it go, like pulling the plug out of a sink.

"Ellie," she says. "Are you okay?"

She isn't aware of standing up, but the stool clatters over beside her.

"Mummy, please come!"

There's fear in Ellie's voice. She's just turned eight years old, and she's terrified. Jenny hears herself let out a sound — the release of breath, a sound that isn't a word. Sue's beside her, seems to scoop her up and deposit her on the other stool.

"Mummy —"

Jenny hears Ellie's throat catch against the word. She grabs for Sue's arm — moves the phone away from her mouth, says, "Call Nick!" and the words tumble out, shrill and panicked. "I'm coming," she says into the phone, and she hears Ellie sob, and a rush of her own breath, and then it sounds as though Ellie's dropped her phone.

"Ellie, can you hear me?" she calls, but Ellie doesn't answer. "I'm coming, don't worry," and there's still no answer.

Behind her, Jenny hears Sue on her own phone, asking for Nick. The final customer's half-risen from his seat, hands open, like he doesn't know whether to offer to help or to leave.

"Ellie, are you there?"

But all Jenny can hear is static on the open line.

***

When Martin Carter presses his foot down against the accelerator, a surge of power thrusts the car forward. His focus is tight on the road, processing every piece of information, anticipating; he barely needs any pressure on the wheel for the steering to respond; it's like the car is in tune with him, responding to his thoughts.

"Still engaged."

Martin glances across at his brother, slumped in the passenger seat. "You said she had Ellie on the phone," he says. "Maybe she's talking to her?"

Nick doesn't reply.

Martin slows the car to take a bend, surges out of the other end. Flashes of images as he drives: the town in new darkness, rain sweeping across blue streets, other cars turning at junctions ahead of them. He's trained for this; he's in that sweet calm centre of absolute concentration.

"Quarry Woods, though," Nick says. "What if —?"

"Nothing'll have happened to her."

Martin hears the authority in his own voice; hopes Nick is convinced by it. They're leaving the town now, plunging into the darkness of country roads, but he's so alert he can feel the way, can almost taste their destination.

Nick mumbles something.

"What?" Martin says, and Nick doesn't repeat it but Martin's hearing is tuned, all his senses are tuned. "This is nothing like Angela," he says. "Nothing like."

"How do you know?"

"Ellie's in the woods, that's all. We'll find her. If we don't find her right away, I'll call Control and we'll get the whole of the fucking Nottinghamshire force out looking, all right?"

Nick doesn't speak. Hunches down in his seat, arms folded across his chest.

"Sorry, sorry," Martin says. "I didn't mean to sound sharp."

"She's my daughter," Nick says. There's something strangled in the way he puts the stress on the word — "My *daughter*."

Martin glances across again, sees Nick's profile as a silhouette against the passenger side window. "She'll be okay," he says, and the fear rises up like a sickness from within him. "She'll be fine," he repeats.

From the brow of the hill, they see the dark mass of Quarry Woods. A car is approaching the car park ahead of them; it has to be Jenny. They drop down the hill, see her headlights swing through the gateway and into the car park, and then her brakelights jolting and bouncing across the churned-up ground.

When they pull up alongside, she's out of the car, leaning against the driver's door, one arm curled across her stomach, the other holding her mobile to her ear.

Nick goes straight to her; hesitates, just short of putting his arms around her. "Anything?" he asks, and she doesn't look at him, just shakes her head.

"Ellie, are you there?" she says into the phone. Her voice sounds frayed; about to break.

Martin looks away, at the shadowy mass of the woods beyond the car park. The darkness seems impenetrable. Keep them motivated, he knows that's key: get them looking before the despair overwhelms them.

There are two torches in his car boot, another in Nick and Jenny's. He tests them, shining the beams onto his hand, but however weak the batteries are they'll have to do. He issues instructions, keeping his voice firm, and he's relieved that neither of them question him. He's a policeman, after all; Christ, they probably think he's been trained for something like this.

They enter the woods in formation; Jenny in the middle with that useless phone to her ear, flanked by Martin and his brother. The trees are sparse, thin, and the ground's covered in a tangle of long grass and scrubby undergrowth. Everything is wet. He can hear water running, rain against the canopy.

"Ellie!" Jenny calls. "Ellie!"

Her voice is high, an edge of hysteria. There's nothing in reply. No sound except the sound of them moving through the woods; twigs breaking underfoot, the brush of wet grass.

"Ellie!" Nick calls. "Ellie, where are you?"

The torch beams play small over the dark ground, giving them nothing more than brilliant glimpses of clumped grass, tree roots, muddy path. They could walk right by Ellie and they'd never see her.

"Ellie! Ellie!" Martin calls, swinging his torch beam in a sweeping arc.

Nothing but the uprights of tree trunks. The wind picks up, sending a rattle of rain down from the branches.

"This way," Martin says.

Nick turns without a word, but Jenny pauses. "Where are we going?"

Her skin is grey in the gloom. Martin can see fear in her expression, can see what it must cost her just to be in these woods. He softens his voice. "You know where we're going," he says.

It's hard work, pushing through the woods in the darkness. The phone is silent at her ear, not even the comforting crackle of static any more, but Jenny doesn't dare take it down, and with the torch in her other hand she's struggling for balance.

Martin is a few paces ahead, taking charge; Nick is focused on the beam of light, the patch of visible ground. For a moment, she thinks that he knows she's looking at him, that he's deliberately avoiding her gaze. She thinks it might be anger holding his body so rigid; maybe he's angry at her, and she can't think why. He's the one who was supposed to be looking after Ellie. She cuts the thought off — this is not the time — and then he does look at her; a quick, reassuring glance that doesn't hide his worry, and she feels a rush of love for him, and the ache that is her love for Ellie rushes in with the feeling.

Ellie, alone, out here in the dark. Jenny can't bear to think of it, presses onwards, strains her ears to hear something — anything — through the mobile phone.

And then, finally, they reach the quarry itself.

It doesn't look like much; perhaps an acre of ground stripped of stone a thousand or more years earlier, so that a hollow crescent now filled with scrubby growth seems to have been bitten out of the wooded hill. There's a sheer drop; at its highest point, almost fifty feet of broken cliff shielded by undernourished trees, casting dark shadows into the curve of the crescent. As they approach from below, Jenny catches a bitter whiff of stagnant water and rotting vegetation.

"You stay back here," Martin says. "Nick and I can do this bit."

She nods, aware that she can barely be seen in the darkness. She doesn't trust her voice. This is the closest she's been to the quarry in seventeen years.

She stands watching the pale flicker of the torch beams as Martin and Nick move through the scrub. The darkness closes in, the top branches of the trees forming spikey black shapes against the paler sky. For the first time, she notices that a chill is working its way into her bones. She draws her jacket tighter around her, waits.

It's Nick who finds the body.

He calls for Martin. He doesn't say what he's found, but there's something about his tone — something about the way their minds are working. She hears Martin hurry towards Nick, but she doesn't move. She doesn't want to move.

She can feel her heartbeat, almost painfully.

Finally, she can bear it no more, and pushes through the scrub into the quarry hollow. She picks out Martin and Nick, their pale clothes and faces visible against the black mass of the overgrown cliff face. They're angling their torch beams upwards, into the lowest branches of the trees. She raises her eyes to follow the light, and she makes sense of what she's seeing just as the two of them turn towards her.

"Who is it?" she asks.

"Carl Blakey," Martin says, almost too quietly for her to hear.

She looks up again, at the man suspended in the torch beams. He must have fallen from the very top of the cliff. He's come down in the trees like a parachutist, tangled up in his wires; feet first and arms twisted in the branches beneath a slack and bloodless face.

"Is he — dead?" she asks.

"Oh yes."

She looks up into the face — the bulging eyes, the tongue pressing from behind the teeth. He looks surprised, staring down at the ground as if shocked by the fall and then shocked again by his sudden halt among the trees, six or seven feet above the quarry floor. The trousers of his grey suit are twisted, one leg caught and pulled up by the branches to reveal a strip of pale skin above a damp and wrinkled sock. One forearm hangs free, swinging slightly, reaching towards her.

"We have to keep looking," Martin says, quietly.

She turns back. Martin's resting his weight on one hip, looking around him with a calculating expression. She has the impression he's remembering procedures, trying to be professional. Next to him, Nick is frowning, and she's struck by the thought that his expression must be a mirror of her own.

"You think Ellie's nearby?" she says, and before Martin can answer, she turns and calls into the darkness: "Ellie! Ellie! Where are you?"

That seems to galvanise Nick. He pushes further into the quarry, thigh-deep in growth, torch beam cast downwards, probing the darkness. Martin heads the other way, looking for the path that climbs to the top of the quarry cliff. Jenny turns back, towards the body hanging in the tree.

"Ellie!" she calls again, but when she listens for a response, all she can hear is Nick beating a path further into the quarry, and his voice, repeating Ellie's name.

The body is grotesque, hanging there. Arms caught up like a marionette. A mass of darkness down his front that might be blood. She lets her torch beam play across the face once more. The head is pressed against a twist of branches, thin and flexible as ropes, pulling and distorting the flesh on one side of the face, giving him an oddly swollen look.

Carl Blakey.

He was always so thin when they were kids; full of that nervous energy that seems to burn all the fat off the bones. Fidgeting his way through class, boney fingers with knuckles that always looked swollen, that later became broken and scarred; a face so thin that when he smiled he seemed to show all of his teeth at once, like his skull was forcing its way out from beneath his skin.

He doesn't look like that now.

"Where's Ellie, you bastard?" she hisses, into the grey, swollen face. He doesn't reply.

She turns the torch, lets the beam run over the cliff wall and the trees behind him. She's about to move away, maybe follow Nick's example and search the long grass, when the torch beam catches a flash of something. There's a patch of darkness like a hollow against the cliff face. She aims the light and sees a glint of something man-made, plastic or vinyl or something else that reflects.

"Ellie!" she calls, but there's no movement.

She has to get higher to see into the hollow. There's a twist of tree roots and low branches at the base of Carl Blakey's tree, and she pulls herself up and reaches forward. The narrow beam of light barely penetrates the hollow, but it doesn't matter. Jenny can see her daughter, on her back, one bare arm flung across her chest. Torn clothes, blood; her face is turned away, but her chest is moving, she's definitely breathing.

"Nick! Martin! I've found her!" Jenny calls. "Over here, over here!"

She looks for a way to climb into the hollow. Her arm is hooked around the narrow trunk of Carl Blakey's tree, and she has to let go to ease her way forward. She's almost level with his loose forearm, that hanging hand with its broken knuckles, and as she shifts her position the tree moves, and Carl Blakey's body gives a lurch and swings towards her. The hand comes at her, soft grey flesh misshapen around the old injury of those broken bones; his body shifts and drops, and as he swings towards her she sees the grey flesh beneath his jaw, loose like a flap. She puts out her hands to ward him off, but he's already falling, taking her with him. The whip-crack of the final branches breaking, tumbling to the ground below, and the air is knocked from her lungs as his weight punches down on top of her. A knee in her thighs, an elbow in her stomach and her head slams down. Darkness folds in and then retreats, and he's solid on top of her, a fleshy mass, dead weight pinning her down. She closes her eyes and screams.

2.

Nick returns from the drinks machine with two plastic cups of coffee and offers one to Jenny. She isn't sure she wants it, but takes it anyway.

Nick says, "She's a fighter. She always has been. She'll pull through this."

They're in a little side room, waiting for news. It's all happened so fast — after finding Ellie in the quarry, there's nothing in Jenny's memory except a blur of flashing lights and yellow neon jackets in the darkness, and then the hospital, and waiting. Her hands shake if she thinks about it, the fear rises through her like sickness — Ellie lying on an operating table, and she can't bear the thought.

Nick says, "What was she even doing there? And with Blakey of all people — what the hell was going on?"

They've been over this ground before. Jenny sips her drink, tries to swallow down that chemical tang of artificial sweetener.

"And Blakey — I mean, it's been years. And at the quarry, of all places. I don't understand."

Again, she doesn't respond. She feels like every drop of disbelief has already been wrung from her.

"I didn't even know he was back in town. Did you?"

For a moment, she considers not telling him, but now isn't the time for hiding anything. "I saw him," she says. "Last Wednesday."

"Last Wednesday?" he repeats, and she knows the significance of the day has not escaped him.

"He came to the café," she says.

"The café? On Wednesday?"

She closes her eyes, presses her fingers against her forehead, waits for him to process the information.

"And you didn't tell me this?"

He's turned away, is standing with his shoulders slightly hunched.

"It didn't mean anything," she says. "He just had some tea and left. We barely spoke to him. It doesn't matter now, does it?"

But he's turning to look at her, and she can see the anger burning there. "Wait a minute," he says. "Wait a minute, rewind, rewind. Ellie was there on Wednesday. You let that fucking paedophile talk to Ellie?"

Rewind, rewind — she wishes she could. She presses her hands to her forehead, rubs her eyes. There are so many things she wishes she could change.

Wednesday had been a day of rain; humming across the tarmac outside the café, hissing in the gutters and down the outside of the windows, playing like radio static in the background.

Sue was serving out front, aided by Ellie; Jenny was in the kitchen, slicing a fresh lasagne into portions, ready for the freezer. The café wasn't busy; the slow drag of a damp off-season, with few tourists risking the weather for a trip into Sherwood Forest, and nobody but lorry drivers and occasional walkers coming into town. Jenny had taken the car to fetch Ellie from school, and apart from other school-run parents, she hadn't seen a soul on the rain-swept streets.

The whole school had smelled of damp clothes warming on radiators, the kids over-excited by a day confined to the classrooms. Some of the mothers had brought dry socks and wellingtons, but Jenny hadn't thought of it.

"Mrs Carter? Could I have a word?"

Jenny had turned, smiled as Ellie's teacher, Miss Baxter, approached her. "Of course," she said, and Miss Baxter jerked her head, urging her away from the children crowding around the parents and the door.

"What's the matter?" Jenny asked, looking back. Ellie was at the centre of the crowd, trying to put on her anorak, turning on the spot as she reached behind her for the second sleeve.

"Maybe it's nothing," Miss Baxter said. "I don't want you to think — well, I'm sure it's nothing, but I thought I'd better say something."

"What?"

Ellie had grabbed the anorak collar between her teeth, was using her mouth to pull the anorak up over her shoulder, her arm thrust outwards, her hand still hidden by the over-long sleeve.

"She's been saying things," Miss Baxter said.

Something in the awkwardness of Miss Baxter's tone made Jenny look at her. She was very young to be a teacher, had only just joined the school; this had to be her first appointment. She wore long skirts, no make-up, an Alice band. There was a suggestion of scrubbed and wholesome activity about her, as if she spent her weekends playing netball and singing in the church choir.

"She seems to have an unhealthy interest in — in bad things that could happen."

Jenny felt her expression tighten, tried to keep the coolness out of her tone. "Such as?" she asked.

"Stranger danger, for one thing."

"That seems like quite a good thing, don't you think?"

Miss Baxter clearly didn't. "She told Chloe that little girls get murdered in the woods," she said. "Chloe got quite upset."

Jenny wanted to say, "Maybe Chloe needs to know these things?" She wanted to say, "Little girls do get murdered in the woods." She wanted to tell Miss Baxter that Ellie might have an interest in the bad things that could happen, but if that kept her safe, how could it be unhealthy? But she didn't say that. She looked back at Ellie, in the centre of a huddle of little girls, talking and laughing, and then she smiled at Miss Baxter. "I'll have a word with her about it."

"Thank you," Miss Baxter said. And then, more brightly, "We don't want them to develop fears, do we? We can't wrap them in cotton wool, after all."

"No, of course not," Jenny said, and turned away. Walked towards the group of children near the door. "Come on, monster," she said, and Ellie grinned but didn't move away. She had taken something from her anorak pocket and was showing it to the girl closest to her.

Chloe, looking wide-eyed into Ellie's cupped hands. Miss Baxter was watching them; Jenny could feel her gaze, like a prickling on her neck. She felt her face flush; the classroom was stifling, there was no air at all.

"Ellie, come on," she said, and her voice was sharper than she intended.

Ellie looked surprised, but didn't argue. She said goodbye to Chloe, and zipped up her anorak, and when they went out towards the car, she even slipped her hand inside Jenny's and gave it a squeeze.

All the way back to the café, Jenny had wondered what to say about Miss Baxter's comments. Had almost started, several times, phrasing the words in her mind — "You know what happened to Angela? Well, it was a horrible thing, but it's very very rare. It was a long time ago and it won't happen again. And some people get upset when we talk about it, so it's best not to mention it at school, okay?"

She hadn't been able to say anything like that. She'd tried, of course she'd tried, but today of all days?

As she stood in the café kitchen, holding the knife over the tray of lasagne, waiting for it to cool enough to slice, she tried to think what she could have said to Ellie. Ellie wasn't daft, she could work things out for herself. It would have been Angela's twenty-eighth birthday today, and Ellie knew that.

Jenny pushed the knife through the centre of the lasagne and drew the blade across, cutting it in half. Oily sauce oozed up to fill the cut. In the café, she could hear Ellie chatting away, telling Sue about her homework. Really, Miss Baxter had nothing to be worried about — Ellie was a perfectly normal child. A little headstrong at times maybe, but since when was that a problem?

The lasagne was still too warm to take out of the tray, so Jenny set aside the knife. She heard Ellie say, "Miss Baxter's really strict, she makes us write out each word in a proper sentence. But I don't mind, it's like telling a story."

"Oh really?" a man's voice said. "What word are you doing now?"

Jenny grinned, headed out to check that Ellie

wasn't annoying the customer. Sue was wiping tables. There was only the one customer in the café, a man in a grey suit, sitting with his back to Jenny. Ellie was standing at his side, her exercise book in her hands.

"The word's 'fractured'," Ellie said. "Like when I broke my arm. That's what it means. Did you break your hands?"

The man gave a soft chuckle, lifting his hands from the table to give Ellie a better look. From behind, Jenny saw the man spread his fingers. Each of his finger joints and his knuckles had been flattened and misshapen, with white scars zig-zagging across the flesh. But she wasn't really focusing on his hands. She was looking at the shape of him, seeking out his younger self in the slope of his shoulders, the shape of his skull. She didn't really need the confirmation; she'd known who he was the moment she heard him laugh.

"Sue," she said, and there must have been something in her tone, because Sue immediately abandoned the table-wiping. "I want you to take Ellie into the kitchen, right now," she said, and Sue gave her a questioning look but moved towards Ellie.

Jenny walked towards the man. He hadn't turned to look at her, was still holding his hands up, but now it was a gesture of surrender.

"Come on," Sue said, reaching for Ellie's shoulders, but Ellie shook her off.

"I don't want to go into the kitchen," Ellie said. "I want to stay here."

Jenny walked slowly around the man. Stood in front of him. She kept her eyes on Ellie. Her actions felt too precise; she felt that she was under scrutiny, that Ellie's shrewd gaze would decipher the situation before Sue could pull her away.

"Just go with Sue, Ellie," Jenny said. Her voice sounded forced. She thought of the sharp knife lying next to the lasagne; wished she had it with her.

Sue gripped Ellie's shoulders more firmly, tried to steer her away. Ellie began to resist; Jenny could see her face screwing up, ready to argue. Then the man said, "Do what your mother says, Ellie. We'll talk again."

Jenny switched her gaze to the man. He lowered his hands, laid them flat on the table. Looked directly at her. He'd put on weight over the years; the skeletal look had almost left his face, the flesh beneath his eyes sagging and grey, like bruises.

"Carl Blakey," she said, and her voice came out almost like a breath. Then the anger caught up with her. "How dare you come here!"

He swallowed his smile. "I had to come," he said. "How could I not come, today of all days?"

She stared at him. She couldn't think of a response.

"I mean," he went on, "it's Angie's birthday — I had to come."

She'd always said he would come back. Year after year she'd said the same thing, and now he finally had returned. Responses rushed into her mind, tumbling one over the next. She found herself stammering.

"You have to know I'm innocent," he said.

Her mind came up hard against the word. "Innocent?" she repeated.

"Yes," he said, and he seemed unaffected by

her disbelief. "You know that, you must do, deep down. You know me, Jenny — we've been friends our entire lives."

"Friends! You killed my sister!"

This time, his smile didn't falter. "How could I hurt Angie?" he asked. His tone was reasoning, gentle, but the way he was looking at her — that unflinching gaze — she wanted to look away, but she couldn't move.

"Angie was one of us," he said. "I couldn't hurt her."

"Sue," she called, her eyes still on Blakey. Knowing Sue was in the kitchen doorway, hearing every word; hoping Sue would play along with the bluff. "Sue, use the phone in the kitchen, call Nick, tell him to bring Martin over, right away."

Blakey smiled, started to rise from his seat.

"He's a policeman now," Jenny said. "Martin, I mean."

Blakey inclined his head, barely a nod. He scraped back his chair, took a step towards her. She backed away, came up hard against another table. A sharp pain in her thigh but she ignored it, keeping her eyes on him.

"I've had a lot of time to think about what happened," he said. "Aren't you interested in what I have to say?"

But she was thinking about Ellie, standing there, chatting to him. How she hadn't realised, how nobody had been able to tell. He'd walked right in here and she hadn't even known he was in town.

"Just get the hell out of here," she said. "You want to still be here when Nick and Martin get here?"

"You haven't called them," he said, but he was moving towards the door.

Jenny glanced towards the kitchen. Sue was in the doorway, trying to shield Ellie; Ellie was having none of it, forcing her way out to see what was happening. A pale face, wide-eyed, too curious for her own good.

Blakey had followed Jenny's gaze. "She's a nice kid," he said, reaching for the door handle. "How old is she now? Eight? Nine?"

"You leave her alone, you bastard!"

Blakey laughed. "Looks just like Angie, doesn't she?"

And then he was gone.

3.

Nick is thinking about Ellie tucked up in bed at home, under her *Princess Barbie* duvet cover. Smiling up at him, hoping for a story.

She isn't like that now. She's unconscious still; they're feeding oxygen into her lungs through pipes in her nostrils, there's a drip in her hand, sensor pads on her chest, a bandage around her head. It's too early to be sure of anything; they're waiting for swelling to go down, for test results, for the next doctor's round.

Jenny is on a chair beside him, next to Ellie's pillow; leaning forward, elbows on her knees, studying Ellie as if every breath could be revealing.

It's been a long fifteen hours since they found Ellie — and Blakey — in Quarry Woods. Nick's head spins with it all. He knows it was touch-and-go for Ellie for a while; remembers a doctor telling him they're through the worst of it, a slap on the arm and big relief and then that same doctor's caution bringing them back — she's not out of the woods yet, but fingers crossed.

Not out of the woods. Jesus.

He rubs a hand over his face, flexes his shoulder muscles, tries to find a comfortable position on the chair but after all this time there isn't one. Jenny glances back at him, scared-eyed; attempts a smile before returning to vigilance.

Nick leans back in the chair, tries hard not to yawn.

All he can think about is Ellie through the years. Ellie newborn, the first time those fingers curled around his, the first time she smiled, talked, walked. Her first day at school; putting her to bed under that *Princess Barbie* duvet cover. She likes to pretend she's a princess, has lots of imagination.

Tell me a story, Daddy. Jesus.

The past is like that — bubbling up when it's least welcome. And Ellie has always known how to take him by surprise.

It wasn't much of a hiding place. Wriggling on her stomach, Ellie could crawl into the gap between the bookcase and the landing wall and peer down between the banisters at the hall below. If anyone looked up from the bottom of the stairs they would see her, but Ellie liked the tightness of the space, and the rush of dizziness that came with looking over the edge at the drop to the carpet below.

Mummy and Daddy were *discussing* in the kitchen. That was what Daddy would call it if she asked him — he would say, "We weren't arguing, poppet, we were *discussing*," and he'd plant a kiss on her forehead and tell her everything was okay.

But it wasn't okay. She'd felt the tension rising inside the house, thickening the atmosphere, like someone turning up the thermostat. A fortnight earlier, Ellie had turned six, and she'd felt so grown up, but ever since then everything seemed wrong. She'd heard Mummy snapping at Daddy, bitter little conversations she wasn't supposed to know about. Sometimes, when she came into a room they stopped talking, and Mummy turned away, and sometimes, Mummy was crying.

Ellie pressed her face against the banister. She heard the tap come on in the kitchen below, water pouring into the sink, the clink of plates being dropped in, one after the other.

Then Mummy said, very distinctly, "What if he turns up this year?"

"He won't," Daddy said. "He's been out for five years, he's only been back that once — why would he come back this year?"

"He said —"

"That was a long time ago."

Daddy's voice seemed to be coming closer. Molly backed out of the hiding place, out of view of the hall. Then she heard the click of the kitchen door being pushed shut. She listened, kneeling on the landing carpet, but couldn't hear their voices any more.

She stayed there very quietly, for what felt

like a long time. Then, without even really thinking about it, she got up and went into Mummy and Daddy's bedroom.

The box was hidden at the back of Mummy's wardrobe. It was a metal box with a stiff, hinged lid, a little smaller than a shoe box, enamelled a watery turquoise that glittered and shifted beneath encrusted glass beads.

There was something dangerous about the box. Ellie had always felt that, even without knowing what the things inside meant.

Ellie crawled into the wardrobe and pulled the door so that it was only open a crack. The shaft of light fell across her knees as she crouched among the shoes, underneath the hems of skirts and dresses hanging on the rail. The air was dry with cotton and linen; she could smell washing powder and perfume and dust. She positioned the metal box in the shaft of light and eased open the lid.

Inside was the little lock of blonde hair, tied up in a faded pink ribbon, and a long strip of purple ribbon wound into a neat bundle, and a small silver cross on a chain. Reaching underneath, Ellie drew out the little pile of photographs.

The first photograph showed a very young girl sitting astride a pink bike. There were stabiliser wheels attached to the bike's rear axle, and pink and purple ribbons tied to the handlebars. The girl was wearing blue jeans and a pink quilted jacket, zipped up to a pink and purple scarf around her neck.

"Angela," Ellie said, trying out the name. It felt strange in her mouth, an unfamiliar shape. She touched the girl's face; the white-blonde hair, just like her own. The girl was smiling, a big enthusiastic smile, as if she didn't know that within a few short years she would be dead.

Ellie knew Angela was dead. She felt like she'd always known that Angela was dead. She couldn't imagine being Angela, sitting on that bike with the pink and purple ribbons, not knowing that she was going to die.

She looked at the next photograph. Angela looked about Ellie's own age. She was sitting on a folding chair, wearing a pale sundress, her hands clasped in her lap, her head tilted slightly to one side. Her eyes, almost hidden in shadow, seemed to be fixed on something other-worldly.

Ellie propped the photograph up against the back of the wardrobe, so that it was illuminated by the strip of light from the door. Looked at the next photograph.

In the kitchen, Nick concentrated on breathing out, slowly. He had his back to Jenny, his hands wrist-deep in the washing up, but he'd been caught out like that before; his reflection in the window above the sink, maybe, or that strange sixth sense that seemed to tune Jenny into his more critical thoughts.

"Blakey's had time to think since then," he said. "He's had time to build a new life. Why would he want to come back?"

She muttered something he didn't catch, and he twisted to look round at her. Her head was lowered.

"What did you say?" he asked, and when she didn't answer he went on, "You have to accept that they let him out, whether you like it or not."

"I know, I know. I just feel he's going to come back this year, that's all."

He smiled. "You feel that every year."

"You think I'm losing it?"

Her voice was even; he couldn't tell if it was an accusation or a genuine question. He took his hands out of the water, took the tea-towel from her and dried his hands. "I think you're tired," he said. "Stress. The nightmares are back, aren't they?"

She gave a half-shrug. "It seems harder every year."

He put the tea-towel down on the counter, wrapped his arms around her shoulders. Looked into her eyes. They were a little pink, glassy, as if she'd rubbed away tears. "We've talked about this, haven't we?" he said. "It's going to get harder, with Ellie getting older. It's bound to remind people. We just have to make sure it doesn't affect Ellie."

"What do you mean? Ellie doesn't understand, how can she? She's only six."

"She's not daft, love."

Jenny broke free of his grasp. "I just want

her to be safe."

"She is safe. Nothing's going to happen to her."

The silence swelled with Jenny's unspoken reply. Her shoulders hunched.

"You go and sit down," Nick said. "I'll put Ellie to bed."

She gave a helpless shrug, but let him guide her into the living room, onto the sofa. He switched on the TV, gave her the remote control. Then he went into the hallway, pulled the living room door closed behind him. Stood there in the gloom, closed his eyes, let the air settle around him.

After a minute, he opened his eyes and started to climb the stairs. The light was on in his and Jenny's bedroom. It shouldn't have been; he'd switched it off after changing out of his work clothes, and Jenny hadn't been upstairs since.

He thought the room was empty, until he saw that Jenny's wardrobe door was slightly ajar. He crept towards it and, letting out a great cartoon roar, threw open the door and lunged into the space at the bottom. Ellie gave a shriek, and he pulled her out and turned her upside down, his arms tight around her stomach. When she gave another yell, this time of laughter, he lowered her towards the floor and let her slide through his grip. She found the carpet with her outstretched hands and collapsed into a heap, giggling up at him.

"What're you up to, monkey?" he asked.

Too late, he saw the turquoise metal box, open, and the photos lying among Jenny's shoes. His expression must have dropped; Ellie stopped giggling.

"What're you doing with those things, Ellie?"

She scrambled across to the wardrobe, started to gather the pictures together. Turned her big eyes towards his. "I was only looking."

"You know who it is in the photos?"

She nodded, her expression serious. Collected the photos from among the shoes and gave him the untidy pile. It was a long time since he'd seen them; since he'd seen any pictures of Angela. He put them back into the metal box, put the box back into the bottom of the wardrobe, turned to face Ellie again.

"Who are these people, though?" Ellie asked.

She was still holding one of the pictures. He put out his hand, but she didn't give it to him; when he reached for it, she pulled it away.

"Tell me who they are," she said.

He'd never thought they'd keep the story from Ellie forever. Not with Jenny freaking out every time Angela's birthday approached; not with Ellie always asking questions; not in such a small town. Already, she'd come home from school with stories about men hiding in the woods. Six years old, and discussing paedophiles and child-killers in the playground.

Nick let out a long breath. "Fine," he said. "I will. Just give me the photo, and get ready for bed, and when you're in bed I'll tell you all about it."

Not an ideal bedtime story, he knew that. Not Jenny's idea of suitable material at all, but she was downstairs.

Ellie turned to head for her own room. Nick caught her arm and she looked back at him. "One thing," he said. "You mustn't tell Mummy that I told you," and she looked at him with an expression that said that she understood.

Footsteps sound in the corridor outside, and Nick jerks his head up, convinced for an awful moment that he's fallen asleep. Ellie is still unconscious, and Jenny is still leaning forward, watching her.

There's a quick knock on the door, and then Martin comes in. They have a private room; just them and the machinery, and the flit of nurses checking charts and machines. Jenny turns to see who it is, and Martin gives them both that grim clench of the lips that isn't quite a smile, that wants to convey sympathy and empathy and hope. Nick's already experienced a lot of that smile.

Martin says, "Any news?"

"We're still waiting."

Martin stands for a moment, hands half out of his pockets, awkward, then jerks his head towards the door.

"Nick, can I have a word?" he says.

Jenny barely reacts. Nick stands, kisses Jenny

on the forehead, then, after a moment of pause, leans over and kisses Ellie too. Her skin feels cool under his lips. She doesn't stir.

Outside, in the corridor, Martin says, "We have to get our stories straight."

Nick frowns. "What stories?"

"About Blakey, of course." Martin lets out a breath. "I've just come from the station. CID are investigating. They want to know who had it in for him."

"For Carl?" Nick can't stop the burst of laughter; it comes out bitter, angry. "What about Ellie? She's the one lying in a hospital bed, fighting for her life. What about why Blakey had it in for her?"

Martin's trying to hush him, looking anxiously up and down the corridor as they talk. There's a nurse at the far end of the corridor, walking away from them, broad hips swaying, and Martin watches her until she's turned the corner, then hisses, "You've got to keep your voice down!"

"Why?" Nick says, increasing the volume slightly, and Martin grabs his arm. "I've got nothing to hide," Nick says.

"Yeah?" Martin says, and his fingers squeeze Nick's arm. "You sure about that? You're the one who was supposed to be looking after Ellie. How'd she end up in the woods, eh? Where were you?"

The chill inside Nick flares into anger. He tries to pull free of Martin's grip, but Martin won't let go. Then the anger is gone, as quickly as it came; Nick feels hollow. "You know where I was," he says. "At home, with her."

"I believe you, of course. But I know what they're saying — CID. They're saying Carl wasn't an accident. He didn't fall over that cliff, he was attacked." Nick looks down, sees the whiteness of Martin's fingers where they grip his sleeve. "They cut his throat, Nick. You know about murder investigations, we've been there before. They'll turn everything upside down. Jenny can't cope with that. And Ellie won't need that stress." Martin shakes his head. "No, we've got to work out how to handle this, you and me. We're here to protect them, aren't we? That's our job, isn't it?"

Nick takes a moment to nod his head.

Martin smiles. "Good." He releases Nick's arm, then gives it a reassuring pat. "Just think about Ellie," he says. "We all want what's best for Ellie, don't we?"

Ellie climbed into bed, and Daddy pulled the duvet over her. She was still holding the photograph she'd taken from the box, and she propped it up against her chest. Daddy sat down on the edge of the bed, close to her. She could hear him breathing, smell his warm skin.

The photograph showed a garden on a bright, sunny day. The grass was brown, like it had been hot for a long time, and in the background Ellie could see the red brick of the back of a house. In the middle of the picture, sitting on a green tartan blanket, smiling up at the camera, was a group of children. The youngest was Angela, cross-legged at the front of the group, in shorts and tee-shirt. Her limbs looked long and skinny, very white in the glare of the photograph. Ranged around her was a group of older children, maybe fourteen or fifteen years old.

Four boys and a girl.

"This was taken on Angela's ninth birthday," Daddy said.

"Who are they all?"

Daddy touched his finger against the photograph, against Angela. "You know who that is, right? Well, who's this, then?" Indicating the other girl.

"Mummy?"

Daddy nodded, and Ellie looked more closely at the smiling girl in the photo. She was seated just behind Angela, one hand resting on the top of her sister's head, touching her golden hair. Mummy was dark haired, and while Angela's golden hair and pale skin seemed to glow at the centre of the photograph, Mummy seemed to be shrinking back into shadow, her face half-obscured by darkness.

"And who are these, over here?"

Daddy was pointing at two of the boys, sitting side by side with arms wrapped around knees, both squinting up at the camera. One was a little darker, a little older, but there wasn't much in it.

Ellie put her finger onto the older, darker one. "That's Uncle Martin," she said. "And the other one's you. Who are these other two?"

"Ah, well." Daddy gave a little smile, a smile edged with sadness, the way Mummy's sometimes was. Ellie waited while he climbed onto the bed beside her, turning onto his side to face her. His arm was heavy across her stomach; his mouth was so close to her ear that she felt his damp breath on her face when he spoke. "This is a secret, Ellie. Promise me you won't tell Mummy."

She looked at the photograph. The skinny boy behind Uncle Martin looked like he wanted to edge out of the photograph, while the bigger boy leaned back on his elbow at the other end of the tartan blanket. "Of course," she said.

"Don't let me down."

She drew her fingers across her lips in imitation of a zip closing. She expected him to smile at that, but he didn't. He was looking at the photograph.

"When Mummy and me and Uncle Martin were little, we all lived on the same street and played together every day. As well as us, there was —"

"Angela."

"Yes, Angela. But there were also two other boys who lived on our street. One was Mark Ashton, and the other was Carl Blakey."

Ellie felt her breath tighten. Carl Blakey. She'd heard that name before, but only ever in whispers. She wasn't supposed to recognise it. She tried not to react; she felt she was on the edge of discovery, like a light was going to be switched on in a room that was always in darkness.

Daddy looked at the photograph for a long time, and Ellie started to wonder if he would ever speak. She didn't dare say anything, in case he changed his mind. He wasn't even looking at her. Finally, he said, "You have to understand, we were all about the same age, except for Angie. She was only little, but we always had to take her with us. And we didn't like that much, I mean, we wanted to do — grown up things. We didn't want this little kid trailing along behind us."

He glanced at Ellie. She didn't say anything.

"We used to go out on our bikes," he went on. She had to concentrate to hear him. "Out to Quarry Woods. Nobody else ever went there. But Angie didn't like it, the woods scared her. Because she couldn't ride her bike as fast as us, sometimes she'd fall behind." Daddy made a little sound, breath escaping from his throat. "Sometimes," he said, voice barely more than a whisper, hot breath against Ellie's cheek, "we'd leave her behind on purpose. We'd cycle round a bend, and we'd hide, and when she thought she was lost, we'd all jump out at her and make her scream."

Ellie frowned. "That doesn't sound like a very nice game."

"No," Daddy said, and frowned. For a moment she thought he'd decided she was too little after all. Then he went on, "It was only meant to be a game. Maybe persuade her not to come with us the next time." He glanced at Ellie, seemed to read something in her expression. "If we'd known, we wouldn't have done it. It was just a game. I know we could be nasty, but — Ellie, you have to understand something."

He reached for her hand, gripped it tight. She wasn't sure what he was doing; wanted to pull her hand away, but she so wanted to know about Angela —

"You have to understand about boys, Ellie," Daddy said. "They're not very nice. They're savages underneath."

His weight pressed against her shoulder; he was leaning in close; she could taste his warmth. He was kneading her hand with his fingers, pressing and turning the skin. She wanted to tell him to stop, pull her hand away, but she didn't dare move.

"Savages," Daddy said. "Who else would tie a little girl to a tree on her ninth birthday and just leave her there? That's what we did, all of us. But it was Carl's idea, we'd never have done it if he hadn't suggested it."

Daddy's face was very close to Ellie's as he talked, but somehow he seemed to be a very long way away. Like he was deep in his thoughts, the way Angela looked in one of those photographs. Ellie waited.

Daddy said, "When Angela didn't come home for dinner, Mummy was sent out to look for her. She found Angela near the tree." He stopped, turned his face away. "Some boys are worse than all the rest, but you can't tell just by looking. You never can tell. The police worked it out, though. It was Carl Blakey who did it."

She could hear him breathing, quick shallow breaths. She squeezed her eyes shut. She wanted to tell him to stop, she didn't like this story any more.

"You have to understand," Daddy said. "Angela was the prettiest little girl anyone had ever seen. She was like one of those porcelain dolls." His voice dropped. "Some boys, when they see something that perfect, they just can't take it. It turns their heads. You know what I mean?"

She didn't, but she didn't dare tell him that.

"Carl went back and told her he'd let her go, but first she had to do something. He told her to get undressed. She thought it was a game, but when she didn't want to play any more, he said she couldn't stop. She tried to run away, and Carl picked up a big rock, and he hit her on the head. He started beating her head with the rock, and he kept doing it, and he didn't stop until he'd smashed her skull in like an egg. Like an egg," he repeated, and he squeezed his hand into a fist, and inside his palm, Ellie felt her own hand squashing, the bones of her fingers pushing together, crushing her flesh.

"Daddy, stop!" she cried, opening her eyes, pulling her hand free.

Daddy looked at her, and for a moment he seemed surprised, or confused, like he'd forgotten that she was even there. Then he jerked his hand away, put it in front of his face, and he stumbled off the bed, staggered back.

He said, "Oh Ellie, oh Ellie," and squeezed his face with both of his hands. Squeezed like he wanted to crush his own skull, and Ellie thought about eggshells breaking, and she suddenly wanted to cry but she didn't cry, she didn't. "I'm sorry, I'm sorry," Daddy said, from behind his hands. "I didn't mean to hurt you."

Her hand still hurt where he'd squeezed it,

she could still feel the pressure he'd put on it. "You didn't really," she said. "It's okay, Daddy."

He stood there, hands still covering his face. His chest was heaving. She watched him; she didn't dare look away. Finally, his breathing calmed and he took his hands away. His cheeks were red; there was sweat on his forehead.

"You promised you wouldn't tell Mummy, didn't you?" Daddy said. "You promised, didn't you?"

Ellie wanted to tell him no, she didn't like this secret. But she heard herself say, "Yes, I promised," and it felt like she had to gasp the words.

Jenny is resting her head on Nick's shoulder, her breathing finally approaching the shallowness of sleep, when Martin returns. It's been several hours; the doctor has visited and left again, and there's still no news. When Martin comes into the room, Nick puts his finger to his lips and Jenny barely stirs.

But Martin glances behind him, and another man dressed in a dark suit follows him into the room. He's older than Martin, taller and broader, seems to wear his size as proof of his rank. Nick hasn't been around too many of Martin's police colleagues, but he instinctively knows that this man is CID.

Nick moves in his seat. Jenny stirs and opens her eyes.

"Detective Inspector Tony Collins," the man says, crossing the room, and he shakes hands with Nick and then with Jenny.

Martin hangs back, watching awkwardly, as if he isn't sure of his role.

Jenny doesn't seem surprised that a Detective Inspector would visit, and turns straight back to focus on Ellie. Nick looks at Martin, trying to read what's happening in the anxiety that has twisted his brother's stance.

Collins says, "Maybe we could have a word outside? With both of you?"

Jenny leans over and kisses Ellie on the forehead, then moves stiffly towards the door. The Inspector leads Nick and Martin after her, into the corridor. There's a window in the door; Jenny leans against the wall and looks through the glass, arms folded across her stomach.

"So," Collins says. "Your brother's filled me in on the — uh — the family history. The sensitivities. You have our thoughts at this difficult time. I want to assure you both that we're doing everything in our power to —"

"To what?" Jenny interrupts. "To find who did this? I'll give you a clue — he's lying in the mortuary, where he belongs."

Nick finds himself turning to look at Collins, trying to read his expression. The man is inscrutable.

"Who was at home with Ellie that afternoon?" Collins asks.

"I was," Nick says. "I was sending emails. I thought she was in her room."

"We found her bike near the woods," Collins says. "Martin here identified it. You didn't see her go out on it?"

"No," Nick says, and it's suddenly hard to swallow. "I would've stopped her. She was in her room."

"You hadn't noticed anyone hanging around the house?"

"What, like Carl Blakey?" Jenny says. Her voice is heavy with something — anger, sarcasm, Nick isn't sure which. "I think we'd have noticed him, don't you?"

"How do you think Ellie ended up in at the quarry, then?"

"Well, obviously Blakey lured her away while Nick wasn't looking," Jenny says, and glances at Nick.

God, he thinks, and something cold grips his stomach. God, she blames me.

"Could she have slipped away on her own?" Collins asks. "Does she know the way to the quarry? Could she have cycled there on her own?"

"Why would she?" Jenny demands. "Why else would she be there, if it wasn't for Blakey? He must have grabbed her, there's no other explanation — I mean — the quarry — Martin, you know what that place means for us! I thought you'd have explained this — Ellie would never go there on her own."

Nick puts his hands over his face. He doesn't want to think about it.

Collins says, "Nick?"

Nick shakes his head.

"She'd never go there on her own," Jenny repeats. "She knows better."

"She likes an adventure," Nick says. "She always has. And she's always been fascinated by — by what happened in the quarry."

"Because you made her think it was a game! You turned it into a creepy bedtime story when she was too young to know any better! Jesus!"

There's something frantic about the way she's talking. Nick can see the strain in her face, a tautness that isn't usually there. He searches for something comforting to say, but his mind comes up blank. "Jenny," he says, and she throws him a look of contempt and turns away, pressing her hands to the glass panel in the door.

Collins and Martin are both watching him. Nick tries to smile; rubs his hand across the back of his neck. Jenny might have turned away, but she's holding herself very stiff, very still, as if she's weighing every little sound.

"This isn't my fault," he says. He wants Jenny

to turn, tell him she doesn't blame him. She doesn't move. He wants to touch her, put his arms around her, but he's afraid that she'll flinch away from him. He coughs, clears his throat, addresses Collins. "This isn't helping anyone," he says. His heart is hammering, but his voice is very steady. "We know what happened. Blakey came after Ellie, he was fascinated by her. He took her up to the quarry."

"There's nothing to suggest that Blakey was anywhere near her," Collins says. "None of his fingerprints on her bike. There's no sign that she was with anyone else."

"But she was found right next to him!" Jenny says, swinging back to face them. "That's ridiculous!"

Collins inclines his head slightly. "The thing is, we know Blakey's fall was no accident. Blakey's throat was cut, he was dead or dying when he went over that cliff. As to Ellie — well, who knows? Maybe it was coincidence that she was there? Maybe she got too close to the edge and just fell? Maybe she saw Blakey and was trying to reach him? Maybe — and like I say, we really don't know — maybe she saw whoever killed Blakey and they tried to shut her up?"

"No!"

The word is a yell that breaks the hush of the corridor, that makes people down the corridor turn towards them. Everyone is looking at Nick. He puts his hands over his face, takes a deep breath. Then he uncovers his face and looks at them all. "There must be some other explanation," he says.

Jenny frowns. "I don't understand."

But Collins is smiling. He says, "I think Nick's saying that the people who most wanted Carl Blakey dead care too much about Ellie to have meant to hurt her when they did it."

4.

"So why do you think Ellie was in the woods, then?" Collins asks.

Over the past half-hour, with just the two of them sitting in the semi-darkness of an unused consultation room, Collins has adopted a sympathetic tone; even seems genuinely concerned about how Jenny's coping. She can't help but be grateful; wipes her eyes with the tissue he's given her, rubs under her nose, tries to think of an answer to his question.

"I mean," he goes on, "it really does look like she cycled out there on her own. Had she ever done that before, to your knowledge?"

She shakes her head.

"Eight years old. It's not impossible. Your husband says she's adventurous?"

She nods, feels another wave of tears filling her eyes, tries to swallow them. She can feel Collins' eyes on her face; wants to dab away the tears again, but not with him watching.

She's sitting on a wooden-armed chair with a plastic and foam seat; he's perched on a trolley, close by. There's blue paper rolled out along the length of the trolley's mattress, ready for a patient. It's daytime beyond the narrow window, but the venetian blinds are closed and the room is gloomy.

"What you said — about Nick telling her what happened to your sister?"

She forces herself to smile. "Oh, you know. Kids. They're always asking questions."

"And you didn't think Nick should answer them?"

She swallows the emotion that's welling up inside her. "Nick adores her," she says. "She's his little girl, he spoils her. What dad doesn't?"

Collins smiles. "He'd do anything for her."

She starts to agree, then frowns. Stops.

"Having kids of your own puts things into perspective," Collins says. "Changes your attitudes. It's natural for parents to be protective."

Jenny doesn't respond. Keeps her eyes lowered, but she can sense him watching her. She doesn't want to think about Nick; about the things he lets Ellie do; about him not noticing Ellie was missing.

"What happened, last time Blakey came back?"

The question is sudden; catches her off-guard. "Nothing," she says, then adds quickly, "When do you mean?"

"What was it, six, seven years ago?"

Her mouth is suddenly dry. She looks blank; holds the expression while he meets her gaze, searches her face. Then he says, "How did Nick feel about Blakey? They were friends, weren't they, when they were younger?"

"We all were."

"He's angry about it," Collins says.

It isn't a question. She gives a little shrug.

Collins leans in a little. She avoids looking at him, but she can sense how close he is. "What do you think Nick would do, if he came across Blakey?"

"Oh, no," she says. "No, he wouldn't."

"But he has a temper?"

She laughs, too quickly. "Who doesn't?"

He pauses; she shifts in her seat, waits. Then he says, "I can't help thinking what a coincidence it is, though — Ellie going to the quarry just at the moment Carl Blakey is murdered there."

Again, it isn't a question, but he lets the silence grow. Jenny tries to think of a response, but it's as if her tears have rusted up her thoughts, she can't seem to come up with any words.

"Ellie may have seen something," Collins says.

"That's why you're here, then? To find out what she saw?"

"It's one reason, yes."

She has the feeling there's something more to his words. She glances at him, quickly; tries to read his expression. "You're worried about her," she says, finally, and the words surprise her.

"Not worried, exactly." He pauses, as if waiting for her to make the connections, and when she doesn't add anything he says, "I just wonder, if she can identify Blakey's killer, what the killer would do about that."

"No," she says. "No, no, no."

"It's such a personal crime," he's saying, and she doesn't want to hear his words, she doesn't want to understand what he's hinting at. "Someone with a personal reason for attacking Blakey. What's Ellie going to tell us when she wakes up? What's the killer willing to do to keep her quiet?"

"No," she says again. "You don't really think — no."

"I'm just putting forward possibilities. It's my job not to trust anyone. You know your family better than I do. They're the ones with the glaring motive."

"You think — you think she's in danger?"

"I can't possibly know, can I? But if she was my daughter, I wouldn't leave her alone if I could help it. Not with anyone."

"No, you're wrong."

67

His expression gives nothing away. "There's how Blakey died, as well," he says. "His throat was cut — more of a stab, really. A right-handed person, facing him. We even know what kind of knife was used. Clever forensics, not that it'll help us much, it was just a kitchen knife. A large one, with an unserrated blade. They're very common. Used a lot in catering businesses, I'm told."

Another pause, and this time her nerve breaks before he forms the obvious question. "None of the knives are missing from the café," she says.

"You keep that close a count on them?"

She nods, sure her voice will betray her. Wipes her eyes with the damp tissue, and her hand shakes as she does so.

She pauses outside Ellie's room, takes a deep breath. Her eyes ache, the skin around them sore and clammy, and she doesn't want Nick and Martin to notice. Through the glass, she sees them talking, heads close together. She pushes the door.

"You think she overheard —?" Martin is saying.

He stops as the door opens. They both look at her, and for a moment she sees — what? Anger? Fear? Then Martin launches himself out of his chair, turning his back on her, and Nick puts his head in his hands.

"What did I overhear?" Jenny asks.

Martin turns at that, and she realises her mistake.

"Ellie, then," she says, and something cold swells in her stomach. "What did Ellie overhear?"

"Nothing," Nick says, but it's more of a groan than a word.

She looks back at Martin.

"We were just saying," he says, moving towards her. "Maybe she saw what happened to Blakey? Who did it, I mean."

She looks at Nick, but his hands are still covering his face. Holding himself very still, like he thinks he won't be noticed if he doesn't move. She says, "Why did she go to the quarry, Nick? You were looking after her. What made her decide to go right then?"

Nick still doesn't move, or speak.

"Kids are always getting ideas," Martin says, and Jenny thinks she detects a warning in his tone.

"Nick?" she says.

He lowers his hands, looks at them. She can see that he's calculating; for a moment, she thinks he'll disagree with his brother. Then he says, "This is what the police do, isn't it? It's what they did last time, remember? Asking strange questions, niggling away at little details until we got so confused we started suspecting each other. We've been here before. We've got to be smarter this time round."

She looks at Martin. The tension has gone out of his body.

"We've got to be smarter," Nick repeats. "For Ellie's sake, right?"

There's a determination in his tone that she hasn't heard for a long time. She hesitates for a moment. Then she nods, forces a smile. "Right," she says.

Nick reaches for her hands, gives them a

reassuring squeeze. Releases them. "So, what did Collins ask you?"

Martin smiles at her, encouraging, but it's Ellie she's thinking about. Ellie in the woods, and Carl Blakey hanging grey in the tree, and that flap of skin on his neck, and those broken hands swinging towards her —

"He was going on about Blakey coming to town," she says. "When he first got released. When Ellie was a baby."

"What did you tell him?"

"Nothing. I didn't even speak to Blakey then. Why would I have?"

They both seem relieved.

"What else could I have said?" she asks.

"That's all there is," Martin says, but he looks at Nick, and Nick looks away. Then Martin adds, "I suppose he wants me now?" Jenny nods, and he makes a show of rearranging his jacket. "Let's see if he asks me the same things, then."

They were quiet all the way out to the meet. Nick didn't know how Martin had arranged it, why Carl Blakey would have agreed to come, but here they were in Martin's wreck of a car, heading for the car park at the back of the supermarket. There was a feeling of unreality to all of this; sweeping through the dark streets, deserted junction after deserted junction, with Martin crouched over the wheel, a cigarette clenched between his fingers and the smoke filling up the car.

Everything had an air of unreality these days. Woken every night by Ellie crying; the guilty slip back into half-sleep if Jenny got up; the semi-conscious stumble out of bed, cold feet onto cold floor, if it was his turn. Change, feed, comfort; taking tours of the darkened house in the early hours, rocking and cooing the solid mass in his arms, whispering to her — "Ellie, my lovely, my darling, please be quiet, please go to sleep." The smell of milky vomit and damp; piles of babygrows and tee-shirts and toy-sized socks steaming on radiators; the stuffed toys and wooden bricks and plastic shapes that cluttered every floor. Sometimes when he was awake he was overcome by the feeling of sleep-walking, and sometimes when he slept he dreamed his way through entire days only to wake and find they hadn't happened yet; his reality slipping and blurring into hallucination.

And here he was, in the early hours, leaving Jenny sleeping, leaving Ellie sleeping, climbing into Martin's car, passing through deserted streets, unnoticed and unreal as ghosts, and Nick didn't know why he was here, didn't know what he'd agreed to, he only knew that he had to come, for Martin, for Ellie.

The supermarket car park was deserted; a flat plain of dark tarmac, marked out with the white lines of empty parking bays, half-lit by the sodium glow of distant streetlights. Martin headed for the supermarket's main entrance, parked across two disabled bays. The building was in darkness.

They got out of the car. Nick moved a few paces away, stood looking around him. There was a chill in the air. He shoved his hands into his jacket pockets, shivered. A few metres away, the supermarket entrance swam with shadows.

Martin had the car's back door open, was leaning in across the back seat.

"What're you looking for?" Nick asked, but Martin didn't answer.

He opened his mouth to repeat the question, but sensed movement behind him — heard footsteps, very fast. He turned. Someone was running straight at him — he started to throw up his arms and the figure slammed into him, head-first; a hard skull against his nose, and a bloom of pain and blood engulfed him, and his knees and then his shoulder hit the ground.

"Bastard!" he heard someone shout, and feet scuffed the tarmac, and there was the grunt of breath. His head pulsed. He put the heel of his hand against his nose, trying to stem the blood-flow, hold back the pain. Martin was wrestling with the figure; hands reaching for each other's throats, feet kicking at each other's legs.

Nick got up, staggered, balanced himself.

The figure was Carl Blakey.

He realised he hadn't considered what it would mean, to see Blakey again. Child killer, he thought. Paedo, pervert, monster, and the knot in his stomach hardened. He looked around, not sure what he wanted — a weapon, a stick, anything.

The car's back door was still open. Nick could see what Martin had been looking for. There was a hammer lying in the footwell.

He reached in, took hold of the hammer's rubber grip. The hammer was heavy, cold, but the weight was nicely balanced, seemed to want to be swung.

Martin had got hold of Blakey's collar, was using it to swing Blakey around, forcing him down to the ground on his back.

"Bastard!" Blakey said, and Nick realised it was Blakey who'd spoken before.

"Hit him!" Martin said. "For fuck's sake, Nick, hit him!"

Martin was pushing his knee into Blakey's stomach; his whole weight was pressing down, but Blakey was struggling to get free. Nick raised the hammer, prepared to swing. Aimed for the side of Blakey's head. Blakey's hair was thinning; there were lines spreading from the corners of his eyes.

"Hit the bastard!" Martin hissed.

And then Blakey looked at Nick, and Nick saw his face properly for the first time. A hardness in the expression, a toughness that came from beneath the skin. But his eyes — pale blue, wide open: in a rush, the years folded back and he could see the features of the boy he'd known. The boy they'd gone to school with, the boy they'd played out with, the boy who lived up the street.

He let the hammer drop to his side.

"What're you waiting for?" Martin demanded, but Nick just shook his head.

"Let him up," he said.

Martin looked at him, then down at Blakey on the ground. He hesitated, but then he released Blakey.

Blakey got to his feet. He was wary still; glancing at Martin as if expecting him to attack. He wore an anorak that was too big for him, jeans smeared with mud.

"What do you want?" Nick asked.

Blakey seemed surprised by the question.

Martin said, "Don't bother. You should've hit

him while you had the chance."

"No," Nick said. He was watching Blakey. "I want to know why he came back. Why he wanted to meet us."

"You know why," Blakey said. There was something sulky in his tone. "You're the ones that framed me."

Whatever Nick had been expecting, that wasn't it. He found himself staring at Blakey, laughter caught in his throat. But Martin didn't seem surprised.

"Yeah, yeah," Martin said, and there was hardness in his tone. "Here it comes. They all have a story, Nick, don't listen to him."

"I've had a lot of time to think about it," Blakey said. "Did you really think I wouldn't work it out?"

"You're dreaming," Martin said.

"You were both in the woods." Blakey had picked up some confidence now. "Either of you could've done it, but I was down at the river at the time — Martin, you know that! I met you on the way, I had my fishing rod, I told you where I was going!"

"Doesn't mean you went there, does it?" Martin said.

Blakey shook his head, impatient. "You're the ones who were in the woods." Martin started to deny it, but Blakey was addressing Nick now. "You know this, don't tell me otherwise! You know what happened, you were there!"

But all Nick could think about was later that day — the police cordoning off the woods, the ambulance in the car park. Jenny's parents running to the edge of the woods, being held back by a policeman; Jenny being brought out by the ambulance crew, such shock on her face. Jenny, later that evening, at her bedroom window, somehow not seeing her friends gathered in the street below.

Blakey said, "For a long time I thought it was a mistake. Martin telling the police I was in the woods — how could he have got his facts so wrong? I thought — I don't know, everything was so confused, remember?" He was talking very fast now, looking at Nick and getting his words out quickly like he thought someone was going to stop him, shut him up. "All those questions, and everyone so upset, we were just kids ourselves, maybe it did get confused? But I have it clear now — Nick, you must remember this! We were all at the tree. And it was Martin's idea to —"

"No!" Martin said. "Don't you dare —"

But Blakey pressed on. "It was Martin's idea to tie her up and leave her there, he was the one, remember? He —"

"That was a joke," Nick said, and even though he spoke quietly, Blakey shut up. Nick's mouth felt very dry. He didn't look at either of them. "That was just a joke," he repeated, and he could see it so clearly — everyone had been laughing, even Angie was laughing, so desperate to be in on the game. So desperate. He closed his eyes. "We all agreed to that," he said. "We all thought it was funny."

He kept his eyes closed. He didn't want to look at the others.

After a pause, Blakey said, "But I didn't go back afterwards. You must remember that. Jenny — she said she'd go back, her and Mark Ashton. We all went home, we were going fishing, but I was the only one who fetched my rods. Martin told the police I wasn't at the river, but I was. I was there for hours, the spot where I always went. Waiting for both of you. For a long time I thought you'd just made a mistake, Martin, you just didn't see me."

"I'd've seen you," Martin said. "You weren't there."

"No! I was there, it's you who wasn't. You were in the woods, both of you —"

Nick didn't want to hear any more. He cut Blakey off. "What about the police, then?" he demanded. "They said it was you."

"Yeah," Martin said. "What about the police, eh? There's no point lying, they investigated! We all know it was you! They found her blood on your clothes!"

"Yeah — in the laundry basket in the bathroom." Blakey waved his hands, like he was trying to wave away the evidence. "Yeah, right. I killed her and then I put my clothes in the basket for my mother to wash. Does that sound likely? Or does it sound like I was framed?"

Nick was hardly listening to them. He felt

like he was hardly there at all. He was thinking about that day still. The woods; the darkness of the quarry; the way the light fell in ribbons through the trees. Walking away with the others; looking back and seeing Angie, seeing her giggle as they left her there.

"Dream on," Martin said. "Some stranger killed her, broke into your house, smeared your clothes in her blood, then dumped them in the laundry basket? And nobody noticed? Yeah, right!"

"Not a stranger," Blakey said. He seemed oddly triumphant. "That's what makes it so obvious. It had to be you two. You were both in and out of my house all the time, either of you could have —"

Nick didn't let him get any further. The hammer was still in his hand; he didn't even think about what he was doing. Angie — beautiful Angie — what that monster had done to her. A rush of anger pulsed through him, and he swung the hammer. He felt it connect, felt the impact in his wrist, and then Blakey was on the ground, curling up, hands protecting his head.

Nick realised that Blakey was afraid, and he felt a squirm of pleasure in his stomach. So he should be, he thought — so he fucking should be.

"Hit him again," Martin said. His voice sounded tight; when Nick looked at him, he was standing over Blakey, staring down at him, and there was a look of savage fury on his face. "Go on, fucking hit him."

Nick raised the hammer again. His wrist hurt from the previous blow. His muscles hurt when he lifted his arm.

"No," Blakey said, and he sounded weak, he suddenly sounded frightened. "Please don't, please don't."

There was blood on Blakey's face, running down from beneath his hair. The flare of anger inside Nick went out.

"Come on," Martin urged. "He hit you, didn't he?"

But Nick shook his head. He felt weak. He felt like that one blow had drained all of his strength. With a shock, he realised that he'd never actually hurt anyone before — he'd had no idea how it would feel. He looked at the hammer in his hand, let it drop to the ground. Turned his back on Martin, on Blakey. He thought about Jenny, about Ellie asleep in her cot. About Angie. Blakey was a killer, and how could that be? How could Blakey have done it — how could anyone? He put his hands over his eyes, realised with a shock that there were tears on his cheeks.

"Don't feel sorry for this scum," he heard Martin say.

All those times he'd thought about hurting Blakey. All those times they'd talked about it, him and Martin, and when it came to it he couldn't do it.

Behind him, he heard Blakey appealing to Martin; a low, pleading voice, appealing to friendship, appealing to old times. Martin was telling him to shut up, was telling him he should never have come back.

Martin had always been stronger than Nick. When they were kids, it was always Martin who decided what to do, it was always Martin who led the way. Nick had assumed it was because he was older, but maybe it wasn't that? Maybe it was something to do with the kinds of people they were?

He heard the swing of the first blow, and it landing; Martin's rush of breath and Blakey crying out. He didn't turn right away. He felt the impact of the second blow in the centre of his stomach; a swell of nausea, and he turned, meaning to stop Martin, meaning to tell him there wasn't any point to it. But when he turned, he didn't say anything. He just stood there.

Blakey was on his knees, hands up to protect himself. As Blakey started to make another plea, Martin swung the hammer, knocking those hands aside, catching Blakey across the jaw. Blakey went down, a spume of blood arcing over him.

Martin stepped around Blakey. He seemed very calm. Blakey's arm was outstretched. Martin touched Blakey's wrist with the tip of his boot. Then he pressed his weight down on Blakey's wrist, and Blakey moaned and raised his head, tried to turn onto his side. Martin weighed the hammer in his hand, looked down at Blakey's hand, pinned under his foot. Then he laughed.

"How's the investigation going?" Martin asks.

He's at the window. The venetian blinds are slightly open; in the car park three floors below, he can see an old woman struggling to help an old man out of a wheelchair and into the front passenger seat of a car. Martin turns back from the window, looks across the gloomy consulting room to where Collins is crammed into a wooden-armed chair. Collins' suit is crumpled; his face has the grey tiredness of someone not used to working through the night.

"You know how these things go," Collins says. "You're on the job. It's slow progress, there's not much to go on at the scene."

Collins' hands are in his lap. He moves them as he speaks, and Martin sees the flash of gold cufflinks, gold watch. The suit is dark blue, single-breasted, with a faint stripe. Not as flashy as some Martin sees on CID backs, but still beyond Martin's pocket. The shoes are polished, the laces neatly knotted. Plain black socks disappear unwrinkled up pressed trouserlegs. The man probably has regulation underpants, Martin thinks; swallows his smile.

"Any sign of a murder weapon?" he asks.

"Not so far. The teams are out."

"They searching as far as the riverbank?"

"They're working on a grid pattern, moving out from the scene."

Martin nods. He wouldn't have used a grid search himself, not on something like this. He'd have gone straight to the riverbank, less than a quarter of a mile away, the most likely drop site. He doesn't say this. It's the usual thing, after all — the suits thinking they know it all, thinking the lads on the ground haven't got a clue.

"How are Jenny and Nick coping?" Collins asks.

Martin shrugs. "They're strong. They'll get through this."

"It must feel like history repeating itself," Collins says. "For Jenny especially."

"I guess."

Outside, the old woman has got the man into the front seat of the car. His legs dangle out of the open doorway. The old woman struggles to fold the wheelchair.

"And you too, of course," Collins says.

Martin doesn't turn back. Keeps watching the car park below. "Reminders are never good," he says. "They were bad times, after Angie died. Jenny's parents were destroyed by it. Both of them dead before Ellie was born." He glances quickly at Collins, looks away again. "Bloody tragedy," he says.

"It can't have been easy for any of you," Collins says.

He moves away from the window to the worktop that runs along the side of the room. There are boxes of latex gloves, of flat wooden tongue depressors and plastic specimen pots. On the shelves above are neat stacks of bandages and dressings and swabs. He wonders why they aren't all locked away; whether anyone would bother to steal this stuff.

"People treated us like freaks for a long time," he says. "Guilt by association — we must have known what Blakey was capable of, he was our friend."

"Did you know?"

"How's anyone supposed to know what's going on in someone else's head?" he says. "We were just kids."

"But people thought you should have?"

He shrugs. There is the end of a glove protruding from the slit in the top of one of the boxes, and he touches the latex, rubs it between his fingers. The surface is slightly powdered. He can smell rubber, suddenly, and it reminds him that the whole building smells of antiseptic. He's been here too long; he's getting used to it.

"It must be hard on Nick," Collins says. "Nobody likes to see their wife suffer."

He shrugs again. He can feel that Collins is watching him. This friendly act — Martin can see right through it, Collins doesn't fool him. The muscles in his jaw tighten; he tries to swallow the tension.

"Your brother must have hated Blakey."

"Oh — no," he says. Looks at Collins, sitting there, so smug in his fancy suit, passing judgement, like he has any idea. "Don't get ideas — Nick isn't like that. Nick wouldn't hurt anyone, he doesn't have it in him."

"Even when his family's being threatened? Even to protect his daughter?"

"He doesn't live in the real world, he just doesn't get how nasty some people can be. Maybe that makes him naive, I dunno. But he'd never hurt anyone."

"You feel strongly about that."

It isn't a question. Collins' eyes are bright; Martin feels that his expression is being searched. He tries to remember what his point was.

"The thing you have to understand," he says. "Me and Nick, we're tight, you know? And Jenny too, of course. We're a tight unit, we look out for each other."

"You'd do anything to protect them."

Martin frowns. "I don't mean that. We're close, that's all."

"A shame you're not married, then."

He feels heat rush into his cheeks. "What's that supposed to mean?"

"Nothing." But there's something smug in Collins' expression, in the way he's sitting there, in that bloody suit. Martin waits. Collins smiles. "I just hope you don't feel left out, that's all. Fifth wheel, you know."

"It's not like that," he says, and his voice feels tight.

"No, I get it," Collins says. There's something in his tone — almost mocking. The muscles in Martin's hands strain; he realises he's bunched them into fists. Releases them, surreptitiously. Collins says, "Maybe you're the only one who could protect them? Nick wouldn't do it, Jenny — well, you couldn't leave it to her, not with the tragedy she's been through. I could understand you wanting to confront Blakey."

"No," Martin says. "That didn't happen."

"Maybe it all got out of hand? Maybe you lost your temper? It's easy to flip over into violence, isn't it?"

"No," Martin says.

"There've been complaints filed against you," Collins says. "Excessive force —"

A laugh escapes him. "Oh, c'mon!" he says. Makes himself laugh again; an unnatural sound. "Those were dropped, no case to answer. Some little scrotes chancing their arm. You were in uniform once, surely you remember how it is?"

"Nevertheless —"

"Nevertheless nothing! You're looking at the wrong person here, pal."

Collins is out of his seat now; something has made him get to his feet. Martin realises with a thrill that he's as tall as Collins, that he could take this man. He can imagine it — Collins going down, sprawled out on the floor. Blood on that suit.

"You need to watch what accusations you throw around, pal," he says, and he thinks he sees a flash of fear in Collins' eyes. The sweet rush of power. He smiles, and he knows it's a sinister smile, he knows he's baring his teeth, and he fixes his eyes on Collins' eyes, and he waits for Collins to back away.

But Collins doesn't. The fear Martin thought he saw seems to have been replaced by something else. Collins doesn't back away; he steps forward, and the tip of his nose is barely a centimetre from the tip of Martin's nose, and Martin's looking into eyes that have taken on a hardness he didn't expect to see.

Collins says, "This is your chance, pal. Tell me what happened out there."

Martin stares into those eyes; dares Collins to speak again.

"Let it all go," Collins says. "That little girl's going to wake up soon. What's she going to say? Who did she see in the woods? You really want to wait till then?"

Martin wants to laugh. He wants to dismiss Collins. He wants to punch that stupid smug face, see him sprawled out on the floor.

He breaks Collins' gaze, takes a step back, moves towards the door.

"Martin," Collins says, and it's a warning.

His heart is beating very fast. His breath hurts in his chest. "Screw you," he says, but the words don't have the force he was looking for. He doesn't dare look into Collins' eyes again. "You've got nothing on me," he says. "I don't need this."

"Martin," Collins says again.

Martin strides to the door, throws it open. Catches a glimpse of Collins, still standing in the centre of the room, and then he's away up the corridor. He isn't sure where he's going. His head swims, pain pulsing behind his eyes, roaring in his ears.

Outside Ellie's room, he finally takes a breath. Stands with his eyes closed, forehead resting against the wall. Cool plaster against hot skin. He can hear people walking along the corridors; the murmur of conversation; phones ringing. He takes more air into his lungs, tries to hold it there.

Eventually, he realises he has to move. He goes to the door to Ellie's room, looks in through the window.

The doctor they saw earlier is back. He's got a clipboard tucked under his arm. Jenny and Nick are standing. Smiling. The doctor shakes their hands.

Martin turns away. Leans back against the wall, sucks in some air.

The door opens and the doctor comes out. He

sees Martin standing there; recognises him.

"Good news," the doctor says. "She should wake up soon."

He nods, forces a smile. "That's great," he says, and it takes all the energy he can find to force those words out.

The doctor smiles and moves on down the corridor. Martin presses the back of his head against the wall, closes his eyes. She's going to be okay, he thinks. He waits, but the tension inside him doesn't release. She's going to wake up, and then people will know what happened, and then it will all be over.

After the doctor has gone, they sit in silence, watching Ellie. Nick puts his arm around Jenny, kisses the top of her head, stays like that, his face pressed into her hair.

Martin isn't yet back from talking to Collins, and Jenny is secretly glad it's just the two of them.

They always have been very close, her and Nick. Sharing everything; thoughts, dreams, desires. And yet — and yet there's always been

Martin. She's never really wanted to think about it — siblings are a difficult terrain, full of unseen fissures that open out into the vast loss of Angela — but she's always known there's a wall there, something she can't breach.

Collins' words have been running through her mind, ever since that conversation in the consulting room. She's wanted to shut them off, but they keep coming back. Nick's right, the police always do this, they have to stick together — but she can't stop herself. She doesn't want any of her suspicions to be true, she doesn't want to ask Nick any questions, but there's Ellie, and she's going to wake up — what will Ellie say?

She looks at Ellie, concentrates on her sleeping form, keeps her voice steady. "When Ellie was a baby and Blakey came back. What happened?"

Nick leans forward, puts his head in his hands. They're all tired; she feels it right into her bones, deep into the centre of her being.

"Does it really matter?" he asks.

"To me it does."

A long moment. Then he says, "You remember what it was like when he was released — nobody wanted him to come back. You didn't want that."

It sounds like an excuse. She waits. She doesn't want to predict his words.

"I'd just become a Dad," Nick says. "What happened to Angie — I had a whole new perspective."

He pauses, another silence that grows.

"What did you do?" she asks, but somehow she already knows. When he starts to tell her, to describe what happened in that supermarket car park, she realises that she doesn't need the details. She finds she's thinking about Carl Blakey's hands; the scars, the strange shape to his knuckles.

"Martin took it hard," Nick says. "Blakey was his best friend, after all."

She nods. She realises that she knows what must have happened at the quarry, when Blakey died. She doesn't need anyone to tell her about that. But Ellie — she still can't understand what happened to Ellie. Nick must know, but he hasn't told her. "And Ellie?" she says. Her voice is faint, weak. "Why did she go to the quarry?"

Nick shrugs, and for a moment she thinks he won't tell her. Then he says, "Martin came over. Said Blakey was back in town. Martin was furious, said he'd arranged to meet Blakey at the quarry, was going to warn him off. Properly, he said."

"You mean —?"

"Christ, you think I knew he was going to kill him? You think I'd have let him out of the house? But you know Martin, he's always had a temper. Maybe he lost control? I didn't think —"

"And Ellie?"

Maybe it's the effect of their daughter's name, but Nick puts his head in his hands again. She takes hold of his wrists and pulls his hands away.

"Tell me," she says, and he won't look at her. But he speaks; reluctantly.

"She must have overheard us arguing," he says. "You know how she's obsessed with Angela. She must have decided to go and see what happened. After that, I dunno. I mean, Martin wouldn't have hurt her, would he? That's obvious, isn't it? He wouldn't ever hurt her."

"Are you sure about that?"

She says the words without really thinking about them. Snaps them out — she's thinking about Ellie, after all; how frightened she must have been.

But Nick jerks away from her. "Of course I'm sure!" he says. "He's my brother!"

"You asked him, did you? If he saw her there? What he did?"

Nick's talking over her, doesn't seem to hear her. "She must have fallen over the cliff. She must have seen Blakey fall and was trying to help him, that's the only explanation, it must have been like that, it must have."

He's got his hands up over his face again, like he thinks he can hide from this. Like he thinks it will all go away. "You said yourself he's got a temper," she says. "He's the one who killed Blakey — what else is he capable of? How do you know what he'd do?"

"No, no, no," he says, into his hands.

"Our daughter!" she says, and she realises

he's hiding tears, but she doesn't feel any sympathy. These brothers — she always thought it was good for Ellie, having a close family. She grabs his arm, shakes him — wants him to face what's happened, but he won't look up. His shoulders rock with sobs and she wants to add to them, heap on the misery, make him feel how she feels. "It's his fault that Ellie's lying in that bed!" she says, and he's engulfed by another wave of sobs. "He put Ellie in that bed!" but he still won't look at her.

She gets up. Goes over to the bed, takes Ellie's hand in hers. Such a small hand, such delicate little fingers. The clear skin of her cheeks, slightly flushed. Eyes lightly closed. A small bubble of saliva on her lips.

There isn't really a decision to be made.

She turns back. Nick's still snivelling into his hands. "You have to tell Collins," she says. "Turn him in."

He looks up, disbelief in his expression. "I can't!"

"He's out of control! He could have killed her!"

"No, he wouldn't —"

"I mean it," she repeats. "It's us or him. You have to turn him in."

"No," he says, but it's not a refusal, she can't believe it's a refusal; it's a cry of anguish. "No, you can't say that — what good would it do?"

"You can ask that, with your daughter lying there unconscious?"

He hides his face again; lets out another sob.

"You let Martin walk all over you," she says. "You can't do that any more. You've got to stand up to him." She's shaking while she speaks; she doesn't know if it's fear or anger but it's overwhelming. "Think about Ellie — you've got to do it for her. Talk to Collins —"

"No! I — I can't. He's my brother, it's just the two of us, we have to look out for each other —"

"I'm your wife," she says. She's surprised by how cold her tone is, but he doesn't seem to notice. There are more tears. He sniffs and gulps, doesn't seem to even realise she's there. She wants him to look at her — she needs him to look at her. She grabs his shoulder — she doesn't mean to hurt him, but there's a fury building inside her, and he cries out and pulls away. "What about me?" she says, and he's rubbing his shoulder, and when he looks at her she sees fear in his eyes. "What about me and Ellie?" she repeats.

"What good would it do?" he says. Misery fills his voice. "Blakey's the child-killer, it was Blakey who killed Angie. There's no doubt about it, they agreed at the trial. Martin didn't have anything to do with that. He's not a monster."

"We're not talking about Blakey," she says. "This isn't about Angie."

He doesn't reply.

It feels as though her thoughts are working too slowly. She can feel the cogs creaking. She feels sick, suddenly. She says, "Are you saying — do you mean — was that Martin?"

"No," Nick says. Groans. He buries his face again. "No, no."

She turns her back on him. She doesn't want to look at him.

Carl Blakey. He'd always said it wasn't him.

And, for the first time in a very long time, she remembers Blakey the way he used to be. Carl. The skinny boy who played football in the street, who knew how to build a campfire, who drew pictures of racing cars in maths lessons. The friendly boy who always talked to Angela, even when the rest of them were busy. All these years, she'd read so much into that — remembered his kindness to Angie and assumed the worst — and what kind of a sister had she been to Angie? What kind of a person didn't even notice who her sister's friends were?

"All these years," she says, and the words come out slowly, as though she has to force each one out of her throat, but she knows she's right. She's never been more certain of anything. "All these years you knew — you had to know — how could you not know? It was Martin, all along! You let Angie's killer carry on like nothing had happened. Oh God — you let him play with Ellie, you let him look after Ellie! How could you do that? How could you do that!"

"It's not like that," he says. "You don't understand."

"I don't even know you," she says. She's looking into his face, but it's like she hasn't ever really looked before, it's like she's looking at a stranger. And then the fury catches up with her — she has her hands on his shoulders, drags him from the chair. "Get out!" she screams. He falls onto the floor — she stands over him, pulling at his arm. "Get out! Get out! Just leave us alone — we don't need you!"

"It's not like that," he repeats, but there's less force in his words. He struggles to get up; he doesn't seem to have much strength. "You don't mean —"

"Just go!" she says. "Get out!"

He does. She watches him leave. She feels drained. She feels that everything has changed. Her legs are weak. She sits down and the exhaustion overwhelms her. Her chest is heaving, her throat is stripped.

He's really gone, he's really gone.

The adrenaline is draining from her system. She can feel everything, suddenly. He's really gone, and she knows she'll never take him back, she'll never let him close again. She can't imagine him not being here, she's never been without him. It's like a void all around her, it's like the temperature has dropped.

5.

The quarry is full of ghosts tonight. Martin can hear their breath in the trees as he walks towards the edge of the quarry cliff. The darkness expands around him, engulfing him, baffling his eyes. He has a torch in his hand but the faint circle of light only seems to thicken the darkness beyond its glow, so he carries it at his side, switched off. There is blackness around his feet, and occasionally his shoes catch on a root or a plant, but he doesn't stumble, doesn't fall. He's operating on senses other than sight tonight.

The cliff edge is a suggestion of smooth shapes before the denser blackness of the drop into the quarry. He sits on crumbling rock, lets his legs hang free above the void. He can just make out the uprights of skinny trees below him, the mesh of fine branches reaching up like they want to receive him, but beyond that the darkness pools. Fifty feet down, he thinks, and it doesn't sound far but he can't see the bottom.

He takes the bottle of whisky from his jacket pocket. Takes a swig. He feels numb — his mind is numb — and yet he can feel everything. He can feel the cold currents stirring the air, and the icy solidity of the rock beneath him, and the shiver of the trees as droplets of water collect on their leaves. He can sense the clouds moving above his head, revealing and then covering a distant moon; he can sense the stars, the turn of the Earth, the suck of gravity holding him in place.

He drinks more of the whisky, finds that he's finished the bottle. He holds it out above the void, lets it slip from his fingers. It plunges straight down, into the darkness, and he watches it go, and it feels like he's pitching forwards after it. A rush of dizziness; he closes his eyes and the world spins, and for a moment he welcomes the feeling, for a moment he's ready to submit to it, he wants to feel himself fall free through the air. Then his fingers find the rock on either side of him, and he presses his hands down, feels crumbling earth and moss and dampness under his palms, sucks in his breath and pushes backwards, away from the edge.

He doesn't want to die.

It comes as a revelation. He doesn't want oblivion, he doesn't want to stop feeling, he doesn't want any of this to end.

He scrambles back, away from the edge. Stumbles back, grabbing tree trunks, pulling himself away. The dizziness overwhelms him again and he falls onto his knees, retches, is sick. The sour burn of whisky in his throat and his nose, and he coughs and spits and retches again.

A sudden breeze moves the trees around him. He opens his eyes, turns onto his side. Everything is blurred, grey. The shadows move around him, between the ghostly trunks of the trees, in among the undergrowth. He can see black shapes, figures, and when he hears the rush of the wind he's sure it's calling to him. All this darkness — he thinks it's calling him, coming for him, waiting to swallow him.

I'm drunk, he thinks. I'm drunk, I'm drunk, and the shadows rise up around him, and he closes his eyes, and he hears himself whimper.

The wind calls him again; words, names carried on someone's breath. He closes his eyes, presses his face down against his arms, presses himself into the ground. He can smell dank earth, whisky.

He wants to focus his thoughts. He wants to get up, walk away. He wants to get out of the woods, back to the town — streetlights, buildings, anywhere where the shadows can't get to him. Where the girls can't get to him. But he can't move. He can hear them now — they're laughing, a distant sound, but he doesn't dare open his eyes. They're closer than they seem; if he opens his eyes, they'll be right there in front of him, they'll swarm around him. A parade of girls, pretty little girls with small bodies, milky limbs, long blonde hair that glints in the moonlight — that glints with something dark, a wet mass of darkness on blonde hair, and their faces — ribbons of blood on distorted faces, wounds gaping open, skulls broken open.

He turns onto his back. His breathing is ragged. He keeps his eyes closed, tries to think about other things.

Angela, Angela, Angela.

He isn't sure if it's the wind or his imagination, but he can hear her name. He doesn't want to think about her. His trembling hands against her smooth white skin — he'd been a fool, he hadn't understood how she would react.

He sits up, quickly. Leans his back against a tree, eyes still closed. His head spins; the sudden sharp pain of the beginnings of a hangover. He didn't think he'd ever have another hangover. He wants to laugh.

Then he hears movement through the undergrowth. For a moment he thinks it's the shadows, they've really come for him, but then he realises it's a person. A real person. He feels laughter bubble up from inside him. He opens his eyes. He can see torchlight, moving towards him.

"Hello?" he says, but his voice has no power.

The light approaches. He's dazzled by it; can't make out the figure carrying it. The light shines into his face and he puts his hands in front of his eyes.

The figure reaches him, crouches down beside him. He lowers his hands. It's Nick. He knew it would be. Nobody else would know where to find him.

"You're drunk," Nick says. There's disgust in his voice. "You've been sick."

"I am sick," he says, and the words make him want to laugh again. He has to make Nick understand: it's vital that Nick understands. But he can't speak. He finds that he's crying, he can't get the words out because he's crying.

"Tell me it was you," Nick says. He's crouched right over Martin but his voice sounds a long way away.

"Oh, Nick, I'm sorry," he says, and his voice is muffled, choked. "I'm so sorry, I'm so sorry."

He tries to stand up, but staggers. Nick grabs him. Strong arms under his arms, pulling him back down, and Nick is behind him, holding him, cradling him. He submits, feels his brother's warmth, the pressure of his brother's body against his own.

"Tell me," Nick says, into Martin's ear. "Tell me Ellie was an accident."

He can't do it. He can't say the words.

"Tell me you didn't mean to hurt her."

"I didn't mean it," he says, and the words come out as gasps, almost choked by his sobs. "She was there, she saw what happened. I was frightened, I only wanted her not to tell. I didn't mean it, I swear to you."

He wants Nick to say something, he wants Nick to tell him everything will be okay, they'll work it out, they'll find a way out. They're brothers, they always help each other out. Family is everything, family is the only thing they have.

Finally, Nick speaks. His voice is a whisper, close into Martin's ear. "It's okay," the voice says. "It's all going to be okay."

Nick's hands are closing over his. He feels Nick's grip enclosing his own; such strength, and he has none left. He can't resist. He submits to the hands, lets them place the object within his own grasp. And then, too late, he sees that his hands are gripping the handle of a knife, the blade turned towards him. He wants to ask a question but he doesn't know what the words should be; he doesn't have any words any more. He's looking down at the knife; watching as the point presses against his chest, over his heart. He feels the pressure against his clothes, and then the sharp prick as the metal touches his skin.

He wants to say, "Don't," but it's too late for that. It's been too late for a very long time.